This book is dedicated to kind and courageous children everywhere.

A Note for Parents and Teachers:

Like all Short Vowel Adventures, **Wet Hen** highlights one short vowel sound, in this case the short "e" sound. We believe this phonics focus helps beginning readers gain skill and confidence. After the story, we've included two Story Starters, just for fun. Story Starters are open-ended questions that can be used as a jumping-off place for conversation, storytelling, and imaginative writing.

At BraveMouse Books we believe the most important part of any reading program is the shared experience of a good story. We hope you'll enjoy Wet Hen with a child you love!

The BraveMouse Team

Wet Hen

by Molly Coxe

BraveMouse Readers

Brave Mouse Books

Hen is wet.
Hen's eggs are wet.
"Help!" says Hen.

"I can help,"
says Hen's friend, Ben.

"Eggs-cellent!" says Hen.

Hen is wet.

Hen's eggs are wet.

"Help!" says Hen.

"I can help,"
says Hen's friend, Ben.

"Eggs-cellent!" says Hen.

Hen is wet.
Hen's eggs are wet.
"Help!" says Hen.

"I can help,"
says Hen's friend, Ben.

"Eggs-cellent!" says Hen.

Hen is wet.

Hen's eggs are wet.

"I give up!" says Hen.

"I will never give up,"
says Ben.

Ben does not give up.
Hen tends her eggs.

Ten wet days go by.

Then twenty.
Hen says,
"It will be wet forever."
"Nothing lasts forever,"
says Ben.

The next day,
Ben says "Hen, look!"

Hen says, "Ben, look!"

"Eggs-cellent!" says Ben.

Ben has a net.
What will Ben get in his net?